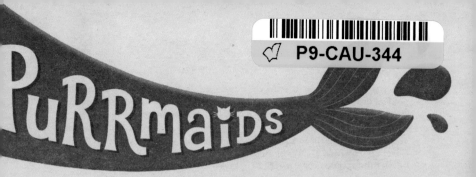

PuRRmaiDs

2 Books in 1!

The Scaredy Cat

The Catfish Club

by Sudipta Bardhan-Quallen
illustrations by Vivien Wu

A STEPPING STONE BOOK™

Random House 🏠 New York

Text copyright © 2017 by Sudipta Bardhan-Quallen
Cover art copyright © 2017 by Andrew Farley
Interior illustrations copyright © 2017 by Vivien Wu

Visit us on the Web!
rhcbooks.com

Educators and librarians, for a variety of teaching tools, visit us at
RHTeachersLibrarians.com

The Library of Congress has cataloged the individual books under the following Control Numbers: 2016033947 (*The Scaredy Cat*), 2016051715 (*The Catfish Club*).

ISBN 978-0-375-97988-0 (Walmart exclusive edition)

Printed in the United States of America
10 9 8 7 6 5 4

2019 Walmart Exclusive Edition

This book has been officially leveled by using the F&P Text Level Gradient™ Leveling System.

Random House Children's Books supports the First Amendment and celebrates the right to read.

Contents

PuRRmaids

1

The Scaredy Cat

Sudipta Bardhan-Quallen

To Rachel, who always helps me create beautiful
things from interesting combinations

It was a paw-sitively beautiful morning in Kittentail Cove. Coral was very excited. After waiting all summer, it was finally the first day of sea school!

Coral carefully brushed her orange fur. She chose a sparkly headband to wear. Then she snapped a bracelet on her paw. It was her favorite because of the golden seashell charm. It matched the ones Angel and Shelly had.

Angel, Shelly, and Coral had been friends fur-ever. They met when they were tiny kittens. On the outside, they looked very different. They often had different ideas about what to do, where to go, and how much trouble they should get into. But somehow their differences made them purr-fect partners. Coral couldn't imagine being without Angel and Shelly.

In fact, one of her favorite things about school was that she got to be with her best friends all day.

Coral grabbed her bag and went to the door. "Bye, Papa! Bye, Mama!" she called. "See you later!"

"Good luck, Coral," Papa answered. "Don't

forget that you, Angel, and Shelly are coming here after school."

"I know, Papa," Coral replied. With a wave goodbye, she swam off. She was meeting Angel and Shelly in Leondra's Square, under the statue of Leondra, the founder of Kittentail Cove.

Purrmaids lived in every part of every ocean. They had towns in coves, reefs, and anywhere else that was beautiful and peaceful. Kittentail Cove was the best purrmaid town in the world! At least, Coral thought so.

"I hope Angel and Shelly are there already!" Coral purred. Shelly was usually on time, but Angel often ran late. The sooner they met up, the sooner they'd get to school to meet their new teacher. Coral was excited to see who it would be.

Besides, the first day of school was a terrible time to be late!

As she swam toward the statue, Coral saw Shelly. Even from far away, Shelly looked lovely. Every strand of her white fur was purr-fectly in place. She had a small starfish clip near her ear, and the golden seashell charm on her bracelet glittered.

"Shelly!" Coral called. "Have you seen Angel?"

Shelly looked up and waved to Coral. She started to say, "No, I haven't—"

"I'm right here!" someone shouted.

It was Angel! Coral spun around to face her friend.

Like Coral and Shelly, Angel was dressed up for the first day of school. She was wearing a necklace of red star-fish. The red looked beautiful against her black-and-white fur. And just like her best friends, Angel wore her golden sea-shell bracelet.

"What are you two waiting for?" Angel asked as she swam past her friends. "We have to swim to school!"

Coral bit back a smile. "You were late— and now you're telling *us* to hurry?"

Shelly laughed. "We'd better catch up. We don't want to miss the bell!"

When the girls arrived at sea school, Angel groaned. "Coral! We're early! No one else is even here yet!"

Coral giggled. "It's better to be early than late."

"But I could have slept longer!" Angel whined.

Shelly patted Angel's paw. "Since we're here, let's find our classroom," she suggested.

Angel scowled for a moment. But then she nodded. "Room Sea-Seven, right?" she asked.

"No, silly." Coral laughed. "That was our classroom *last* year!"

"We're in Eel-Twelve this year," Shelly added.

They made their way toward Eel-Twelve. There was a purrmaid inside the classroom when they arrived. She didn't look like most of the purrmaids in town. Her long fur was dyed every color of the rainbow. She wore three earrings on her left ear and four on her right. Even her tail was decorated with shiny rings!

"Is that our *teacher*?" Angel whispered.

"I think so," Coral answered.

"I've never seen a teacher who looks like that," Shelly said. "She's so cool!"

"Let's go meet her!" Angel suggested.

The girls swam into the classroom. The colorful purrmaid had her back to the door, but she spun around as the girls entered. "I thought I heard some curious little kittens," she said. "You're here early. You must love school!"

"We do!" said all three friends at once.

Their teacher grinned. "I'm glad to hear that. I'm Ms. Harbor, and today is my first day, too."

"I'm Coral," said Coral, "and these are my friends, Angel and Shelly."

"It's lovely to meet you all," Ms. Harbor purred.

The bell rang, so the purrmaids swam to their clamshell seats. Ms. Harbor welcomed more students into the classroom. Then she swam to her giant scallop-shell teacher's chair. "Let's begin, class!" she said.

There was so much to do on the first day of school that Coral lost track of time. She was surprised when Ms. Harbor announced, "Our first day is almost over, but I have some homework for you tonight."

All the students groaned. "Homework!" Angel said. "Already?"

Ms. Harbor held her paws up for silence. "This homework isn't hard, I purr-omise. In fact, you might enjoy it." She floated to the middle of the classroom. "I want to tell you something about me. I love curiosity! Curious purrmaids are not afraid to learn. That's how you find the most interesting things in the ocean!"

Coral nodded. She loved exploring the ocean, too—as long as the exploring part wasn't too scary.

"I am very excited to be your teacher this year," Ms. Harbor continued. "We are going to have a fin-tastic time learning from each other and making waves in Kittentail Cove! To start our year, I'd like each of you to bring something special to class tomorrow."

"What do you mean by 'special'?" Angel asked.

"It can be anything you want!" Ms. Harbor laughed. "Your favorite shell, a beautiful pearl, a pet sea horse. Whatever will show me how you see life's beauty. Help me learn about you!"

2

Coral always felt like she had to swim twice as fast to keep up with Angel and Shelly. But on the way home from school, it was a lot harder than usual. Angel zipped through the streets toward Coral's house so quickly that even Shelly fell behind.

"Slow down, Angel!" Shelly shouted. But Angel didn't stop.

"Don't even try," Coral said. "Angel is excited about something. And when she's excited, nothing makes her slow down!"

"What do you think is going on?" Shelly asked.

Coral shrugged. "I don't know. But I bet it has to do with our homework."

Angel didn't wait for Coral to finish hugging Mama before she asked a question. "What are you two going to do about the homework assignment?"

"Hello to you, too, Angel," Mama said.

Angel mumbled, "Hello, Mrs. Marsh."

Mama smiled. "The first day of school must have gone really well if you are this excited about homework!"

"It did!" the friends answered at the same time.

"I'm glad," Mama said. "Have fun doing your homework."

Coral kissed Mama's cheek. Then she waved for her friends to follow her to her bedroom. "This is what I'm going to bring," she announced. She held up a pink pointy turret shell. "This one is my favorite."

"It's beautiful," Shelly cooed.

"How about you?" Coral asked.

Shelly scratched her head. "I'm not sure. Maybe my red sea-glass necklace?"

Coral grinned. "I've never seen anyone else with sea glass that color. I think that would be purr-fect!"

Angel frowned. "We can't just bring in seashells and sea glass!" she moaned. "We need something better!"

Coral and Shelly looked at each other. "Like what, Angel?" Coral asked.

"I don't know. But it has to be really different and special," Angel replied.

"What if we look around Leondra's Square today?" Shelly suggested. "We could each find something new."

"That's a great idea!" Coral agreed.

"No, it's not!" Angel cried. "Remember what Ms. Harbor said about curiosity? And about finding the most interesting things in the ocean?"

Her friends nodded.

"We aren't going to find anything amazing in Leondra's Square!" Angel continued. "We want things that the other purrmaids won't be able to find. We have to look somewhere no one else will think to look."

"But where are we supposed to go?" Shelly asked.

"I don't know," Angel replied.

"Let's have a snack," Coral said, "and we can think about it."

The girls swam into the kitchen. Mama had set out some of Coral's favorite sushi to share with her best friends. They floated around the counter and popped the sushi into their mouths with their paws.

"Don't let Mama see us," Coral said between bites. "She likes us to eat at the table."

Angel rolled her eyes. "Coral," she moaned.

"I'm sorry!" Coral sighed. "I don't like breaking the rules!"

Shelly and Angel laughed. They already knew that about their friend. Coral was definitely the most careful one in their group. Angel, on the other paw, wasn't much like her name at all. She loved to bend the rules. Shelly liked adventure, too—but not if it meant getting her paws dirty, and only when she didn't have to break *too* many rules.

Angel popped another piece of sushi into her mouth. Then her face lit up. "I have an idea!" she cried. "If we head out to the edges of Kittentail

Cove, there will be lots to discover. We can search Tortoiseshell Reef for something to bring to school!"

Coral gulped. Kittentail Cove was a big place, and Tortoiseshell Reef was as far away from home as they could go. Angel's plans were always exciting, but they were also complicated—and sometimes dangerous. From the way Angel was grinning, Coral knew that this plan would be no different.

"Maybe we should think about this some more," Coral began. "I mean . . . it might not be safe to go so far. There could be strong currents! And it's really close to where barracudas and giant squids and sharks hang out!"

"We'll stay away from the sharks, silly!" Angel answered. "You're paw-some at avoiding danger, right?"

Shelly agreed with Angel. But Coral shook her head and said, "I don't think this is a good idea."

"Okay! Okay!" Angel huffed. "If you don't want to try, we'll do something else."

Coral clenched her paws. "I do want to try!" she yowled. "I'm just afraid of what could happen. Haven't you ever been scared, Angel?"

Shelly swam between Coral and Angel. "You two shouldn't fight. We're best friends!" She turned to Angel and said, "It is a really great idea to search away from the center of Kittentail Cove. I bet Ms. Harbor would be really impressed by that. But Coral has a good point, too. Maybe we should think about this some more."

Shelly smiled, but Coral could see that she really wanted to go along with Angel's plan.

Then Angel said, "Well, if Coral's too much of a scaredy cat—"

"No! I can do this," Coral interrupted. She pictured Tortoiseshell Reef. She didn't know what was out there. But she was going to be brave, no matter how scary it was!

"Are you sure?" Shelly asked.

"Yes, I'm sure," Coral replied.

"Good," Angel said, "because meow is the time."

Ms. Harbor expected them to bring in something interesting tomorrow. Angel was right—it was meow or never.

"I'll race you to Tortoiseshell Reef!" Coral shouted. "Last one there is a rotten skeg!"

Coral zipped through the water. Angel and Shelly followed on her tail. In just a few minutes, they had passed Leondra's Square and were zooming toward Cove Council Hall. At first, Coral was purring with excitement. But the farther she got from home, the more butterfly fish fluttered in her tummy. What if something bad happened? What if there was a cat-tastrophe?

She tried to stop worrying. *I need to have a paw-sitive attitude,* she thought. *We're doing our homework. And then we're going straight home!*

As they reached Cove Council Hall, they saw Angel's mother, Mrs. Shore, speaking to Mayor Rivers. "Mommy!" Angel cried. She darted toward her mother to give her a hug. But she was going so fast that she spun Mrs. Shore around three times!

"Angel!" Mrs. Shore yelped. "Slow down!"

Mayor Rivers chuckled as he helped Mrs. Shore find her balance. "Angel, you've grown so big!" he said.

"And look at you two!" Mrs. Shore said to Coral and Shelly. She took their paws and gave them a squeeze. "How was the first day of school?"

"Purr-fect!" Coral replied. Angel and Shelly nodded in agreement.

"Our new teacher is Ms. Harbor," Shelly said.

"And she gave us a cool homework assignment!" Angel added. "We're supposed to bring something really special to class tomorrow."

"Is that why you're swimming so fast?" Mayor Rivers asked. "We have speed limits in this town, you know!"

Angel, Shelly, and Coral grinned. "We're going to Tortoiseshell Reef to see what interesting things we can find," Shelly said.

Mayor Rivers smiled. "I remember spending hours exploring Tortoiseshell Reef as a youth! If the reef is like it used to be, you will have lots of luck."

The girls giggled. Coral knew what her friends were thinking. Mayor Rivers was so *old*. Back in his youth, the reef must have been just a few elkhorns and sea fans!

"You know," Mrs. Shore said, "usually the most special things are the ones we hold close to our hearts."

"Does that mean we shouldn't go to Tortoiseshell Reef?" Coral asked.

"But, Mommy," Angel whined, "none of us have anything that is truly special at home! We have to go to Tortoiseshell Reef to search!" She clasped her paws and begged. "Please?"

"Just remember not to stay out too late," Mrs. Shore said. "It gets dark quicker at the edges of the cove. And the South Canary Current can get crowded in the evening." She pointed to the tall clock tower that topped Cove Council Hall. "You should all be home before dinner."

The South Canary Current flowed right past the entrance of Kittentail Cove. Most sea creatures used the current systems to get around the ocean quickly. When her parents took Coral to visit her cousins in other purrmaid towns, they used the South Canary Current. But Coral had forgotten that the current ran along the border of Tortoiseshell Reef.

"We'll be careful, Mrs. Shore," Shelly said.

"And we'll be back by dinnertime," Angel said.

"Good," Mrs. Shore replied. "I don't want you to run into any trouble on your adventure."

Coral gulped. That's what she was afraid of, too! But there was no way she was going to say so. She didn't want to be called a scaredy cat again.

"We won't, Mommy!" Angel agreed.

The three purrmaids swam off. Soon they arrived at Tortoiseshell Reef. They gazed around at the beautiful scenery.

"Don't you just love it here?" Shelly whispered.

Coral nodded. There were houses all over Kittentail Cove. Most purrmaids lived near Leondra's Square like Coral, Shelly, and Angel. Some lived farther out, especially the pearl farmers. There were many offices and restaurants near Cove Council Hall. Coral's father worked in one of those offices. So did Angel's mother. Shelly's parents had a restaurant there, too. But no one was allowed to build on Tortoiseshell Reef. The purrmaids of Kittentail Cove set it aside as a place to enjoy the ocean's natural beauty.

"I don't know why we don't come here more often," Angel said. She darted behind an elkhorn and disappeared.

"Angel?" Coral called. "Where are you?"

Angel popped up from behind a huge sea fan. "Here I am!" she shouted.

Coral yelped and hid behind Shelly.

"Coral!" Angel said. "You weren't scared, were you?"

"Of course I wasn't scared," Coral lied, "just surprised."

Shelly patted Coral's paw and said, "It's all right. Angel surprised me, too."

"I'm sorry," Angel apologized. She put her paw around Coral and led her toward the sea fan. "Can you help me with something?" she asked. When Coral nodded, Angel said, "I don't remember all the different creatures who live here in Tortoiseshell Reef. You know them better than I do. Will you show me?"

Coral smiled. Angel was a good friend. Together, they swam toward the floor of the reef. Coral pointed out different animals.

"That's a butterfly fish," Coral said. "And that is a cleaner shrimp."

"Cleaner than what?" Angel joked. The two purrmaids giggled.

"Look over here!" Shelly called. She was looking at something hiding inside a sea whip.

Coral swam closer to get a better look. She saw a beautiful orange-and-white fish zipping between the fronds of the sea whip. "It's a clown fish!" she whispered.

"Where's the rest of the circus?" Shelly laughed.

The clown fish didn't find the joke very funny. He swam away.

The purrmaids paddled slowly around the reef. Coral showed her friends all sorts of animals and plants. She spotted a family of sea horses. "Let's take a closer look," Coral suggested.

"Great idea!" Shelly agreed.

Coral looked over her shoulder. She started to wave to Angel. But Angel wasn't there!

Coral gasped. "Where is she?"

Shelly spun around. Coral knew she couldn't see Angel, either.

"Angel!" Coral yelled. "Where are you?" Her heart began to pound. *I knew something terrible would happen,* she thought.

Coral and Shelly kept shouting their friend's name. Finally, they reached the edge of Tortoiseshell Reef. The coral there had formed a deep tunnel. "Be careful near the tunnel," Coral warned Shelly. "Sometimes eels live in those!"

Suddenly, something came whooshing out of the tunnel. Without thinking, Coral swam in front of Shelly. She closed her eyes and braced herself for whatever was coming her way.

Then Coral heard giggling. She opened one eye. "Angel!" she yelped. "You scared me!"

"You scared me, too," Shelly added.

"We thought you were an eel!" Coral said. She was still trembling from fear.

"If you thought I was an eel," Angel said, "why did you swim in front of Shelly instead of swimming away?"

"I was—I was trying to protect her," Coral stammered.

Angel grinned. "You're not such a scaredy cat after all!"

Shelly gave Coral a hug. "That was pretty brave, Coral."

Coral smiled. "I guess it was," she said.

"Well, I have something else for you to be brave about," Angel said. She pointed to the tunnel. "It's the coolest thing. On the other side of the tunnel, there's a geyser that spins you head over tail. If you swim through really fast, it will flip you over and turn you around. Then you can swim back."

"That sounds so exciting!" Shelly said.

"Let's all do it!" Angel suggested.

"I—I don't know." Coral pulled back from her friends. "What if I can't do it and get stuck upside down? What if I sink? What if . . . ?" She hung her head in embarrassment.

"Haven't you ever tried a flip?" Angel asked. "I've been doing them since I was the size of a minnow!"

Coral felt as small as a grain of sand on the ocean floor. "No, I guess I haven't ever tried."

"We can help you," Angel offered.

"That's what friends do," Shelly added.

Coral sighed. "I don't think I could start by swimming the tunnel," she said.

"You don't have to!" Angel cried. She took Coral's paw. "Let's go over here." She led them to an open part of the ocean. "There's plenty of room to flip here!"

Coral gulped. "What do I do first?"

Shelly and Angel took turns showing Coral how to do underwater flips. "Look at me!" Angel yowled. She flipped easily, over and over again.

"The trick is to swim as fast as you can before you start the flip," Shelly said. She swam into the open water and did a flawless flip. "That way you have the oomph to get all the way around."

Coral narrowed her eyes. She shook her tail out to get loose. Then she started to swim.

Shelly said to go fast, so Coral swam with all her might. Then she tucked her head down and threw her tail back, just like Angel and Shelly had shown her.

And she did it!

Coral was catching her breath when Angel and Shelly swam up to her. "That was purr-fect!" Angel cried.

"You got it on the first try!" Shelly added.

Coral couldn't believe it! "That wasn't scary," she said.

"Do you want to try again?" Angel asked.

Coral nodded. "Yes, I do!"

The girls swam through the clear blue water. They took turns doing flips. Soon Coral couldn't remember why she had ever been afraid. "This is so much fun!" she shouted.

"I need a break!" Angel said. She plopped down on a rock. "I'm just going to sit here for a minute."

"Good idea," Shelly said. She sat down next to Angel.

Coral was tired, too. There was no room left on that rock, so she looked around for someplace else to rest.

That's when she realized nothing looked familiar. "Hey!" she shouted. "Do you know where we are? Because this is definitely not Kittentail Cove!"

"What do you mean, this isn't Kittentail Cove?" Angel asked.

"We're not allowed to leave the cove!" Shelly cried. "Where are we?"

"I don't know," Coral moaned. She bit her lip. "I wasn't paying attention while we were swimming and flipping."

"Neither was I," Shelly groaned.

Angel looked worried. "We're going to

be in so much trouble!" she said. "How are we going to get home?"

If there were little butterfly fish fluttering in Coral's tummy earlier, now it felt like big blue whales! She couldn't remember ever being this nervous. "We need to stay calm!" she said. "We just need to look around. I'm sure we'll see something familiar soon. And then we'll hurry home!"

"Good plan," Shelly agreed. "Should we split up? That way we can see more of the ocean at once."

Angel shook her head. "I don't want to be alone out here! I think it's better for us to stay together."

For once, Coral agreed with Angel's plan. She nodded and said, "Come on. Let's try to retrace our swim."

The three purrmaids moved slowly through the water. They couldn't see Tortoiseshell Reef from where they were. All there was up ahead was a giant kelp forest.

Every moment they were lost made Coral worry more. *What are we going to do?* she thought.

Coral, Shelly, and Angel were very busy trying to find their way home. So they didn't notice the school of fish swimming toward them until they were surrounded by a hundred bright-green parrot fish.

Suddenly, Coral remembered something. "The South Canary Current!" she shouted. "Maybe these fish are headed there!"

Shelly's face lit up. "If we can find the South Canary Current . . ."

". . . it will take us home to Kittentail Cove!" Coral finished.

"You are so smart!" Angel applauded. "I knew there was nothing to worry about!"

Coral rolled her eyes. Angel had *definitely* been worried! "Let's follow those fish," she said.

There were so many parrot fish, they formed a green cloud. That made it easy to follow them without spooking them. Soon Shelly cried, "Look over there! It's the South Canary Current!"

A line of fish, turtles, and other sea creatures traveled in the flow of the South

Canary Current. It was like a high-speed highway for ocean folks. "We'll be home in no time!" Coral cheered. She started to swim toward the current.

But Angel grabbed Coral's paw. "Don't!" she yelled.

"Why?" Coral asked. "We have to go!"

Angel wouldn't let go. She pointed at the water in front of them. "Does that look like smooth sailing to you?"

Coral scowled. "I don't understand."

"Look closely," Angel urged.

"Is that a swarm of jellyfish up ahead?" Shelly gasped.

"I think it is," Angel said. Jellyfish were pretty harmless to purrmaids—unless they got stuck in a big group of them. One sting wasn't so bad, but getting stung over and over was not a good idea. "We can't go straight to the current."

"We have to find a way to go around them," Coral agreed.

"But they're everywhere," Shelly said. She was right. As the girls swam closer, they saw that the cloud of jellyfish stretched over most of the ocean. It was in front of them, from the top of the kelp forest almost to the surface of the water.

Angel pointed downward at the kelp forest. "If we can't go up, we'll go down."

Shelly shrugged. Coral frowned. But then they both nodded.

"I'll go first," Angel said. She swam toward the kelp. Shelly followed on her tail.

Coral hesitated. She was trying to be brave in front of her friends. But she felt nervous. *Who knew what was hiding in all that kelp?*

"Come on, Coral!" Shelly said.

"It's not so bad," Angel added. "Don't be a scaredy cat!"

Coral lowered her eyes. She didn't mean to be scared. She just liked doing things the safe way. The safe way never involved sharks or jellyfish or getting grounded. But now the safe way seemed to be through the forest. She gulped, then shouted, "I'm coming!"

The three friends entered the kelp forest together. There were a few natural passages that let them swim freely. But in other parts of the forest, the girls had to use their paws to part the kelp in order to get through.

"How do we know if we're going the right way?" Shelly asked.

Coral looked up. She tried to catch a glimpse of the South Canary Current, but all she could see was kelp. "I don't know," she answered.

"Let's keep moving," Angel suggested.

Coral nodded. She pushed aside a large kelp leaf. "Wow!" she cried.

"What is it?" Shelly asked. She shrank behind Angel. "Is it dangerous?"

Coral grinned. "No! It's the way out!" She held the kelp aside so her friends could swim through. They were back in the open ocean!

"Where's the current?" Angel looked around.

"It's up there!" Shelly said. "And I don't see any jellyfish, either!"

"Let's go!" Angel cried.

But Coral didn't move. She was staring at a trench in front of them. When she looked down, the water was darkened by shadows.

Coral thought something was lodged in the sand at the bottom of the trench. At first, it looked like a whale resting on the ocean floor. But then she realized it wasn't a living creature. "We've found a shipwreck!"

"I can't believe it!" Coral whispered. "I've read about shipwrecks. But I've never seen one!"

"That's because you never leave Kittentail Cove," Angel purred.

Coral scowled at Angel. But when she saw Angel's face, she knew her friend was kidding.

"Speaking of Kittentail Cove," Shelly said, "it's time for us to get back."

"I want to tell everyone at home about what we found!" Angel said.

"Wait!" Coral shouted. She gazed down at the shadowy ship. All afternoon, every time she had gotten scared, she had made herself be brave. If she could do it one more time, she and her friends could find something truly paw-some. "We have to explore the shipwreck first!"

Shelly's eyes grew wide, and Angel's jaw looked like it was going to fall off. "What did you say?" Angel sputtered.

"The South Canary Current will get us home in a flash," Coral said. "So I think we have a little bit of time. Just a quick look won't hurt, right?" She smiled. "Maybe we'll find something in the shipwreck to bring to school."

"That would be fin-tastic!" Angel said. She shrugged. "I guess I'm in!"

"Me too," Shelly said. "We won't get a chance like this again."

Coral started to swim down into the trench. Angel and Shelly swam beside her. "We can't explore for too long," she said.

"There's the Coral we know and love!" Shelly laughed.

"I'm serious!" Coral added. "We have to be home soon. I don't want to—"

"Get grounded," Angel said. "We know, we know."

Shelly elbowed Coral playfully. "We'll just take a quick peek." She flipped in the water, grinning. "This is so cool!"

The purrmaids swam closer to the ship. It had sunk down into the sand and was tipped over to one side. Giant barnacles covered the hull. Tattered bits of sail hung from the masts. There were holes scattered

around the deck. Beams of sunlight shone down to light different parts of the ship.

Coral peeked in a jagged hole to see into the ship's hold. A small fish swam out toward her. The hold was too dark to see very far. "This is scarier up close," she whispered.

"Do you want to go inside?" Angel asked.

Coral gulped. She didn't know if she could be brave enough to do that. But then she noticed a fancy door. It didn't look as creepy as the hold. She pointed. "Let's look there instead," she suggested.

All three girls had to yank on the handle to get it open.

"I hope this is worth it," Angel muttered.

Shelly peered through the door. "It's worth it!" she shouted, and raced ahead.

The room behind the door must have belonged to the captain of the ship. The floor and the walls were dotted with holes just like on the deck outside. Shelly swam straight to a large table nailed to the floor in the middle of the room. Angel studied the giant globe on one side of the room. Coral saw that the floor was littered with barrels, coils of rope, and tangles of seaweed. She took the lid off one of the barrels.

Something popped out and Coral squealed. "Yikes!"

Immediately, Angel and Shelly came to her side. "What happened?" Angel asked.

"That little guy scared me!" Coral said. A small crab scuttled away.

The girls giggled. Then Shelly said, "Come over here!" She led her friends back to the table. "Look what I found!" She held up a small golden tube. When she pulled on one end of the tube, it extended to be longer than Shelly's whole arm.

"What is it?" Angel asked.

"I think it's a spyglass," Shelly said.

Coral nodded. "Human sailors use these to see things far away," she said.

"I've never actually seen one," Shelly said.

"So it's purr-fect to show Ms. Harbor!" Angel grinned from ear to ear.

"One down, two to go!" Coral laughed. She put one paw around Angel's waist and the other around Shelly's. She hugged them tightly. "Let's see what else we can find!"

Angel's face lit up. "Actually, I have something to show you, too." She swam back to the globe.

Coral frowned. "Hey, Angel, you know that is way too heavy for us to carry home, right? Even if it wasn't nailed to the floor!"

"I know, Coral." Angel laughed. "I wasn't talking about the globe. I wanted to show you this." She held out her paw.

Coral swam closer to examine a small silver circle. She noticed a tiny needle under a glass cover, pointing at the letter N. "You found a compass!" she cried.

"It still works, too!" Angel turned around and waved the compass. She held it out again. The needle spun and pointed to N for north.

"It's paw-some, Angel," Shelly said.

"I'm bringing this to school tomorrow,"

Angel said. "That spyglass and this compass are purr-fect treasures from a shipwreck!"

Coral smiled, but she didn't feel completely happy. *Angel and Shelly found fabulous treasures to share with Ms. Harbor tomorrow,* she thought. *But I still have nothing. And it was* my *idea to come here in the first place. It's not fair!*

Shelly had the same thought. "Angel and I have our special things," she said. "We just need to find something for you, Coral."

Coral nodded. But there was nothing else in the captain's room that she could bring to school. Then she had an idea. "We still have the hold to search!" she cried. She pointed to a hole in the floor. "We can get down through here."

"I thought you said it was scary in there," Angel said.

Coral shrugged. "You keep saying not to be a scaredy cat. And we've been fine so far." She darted through the hole in the floor. "See if you two can keep up with me!"

The floor of the hold was covered in sand, seaweed, and coral. It was like being in an underwater cave instead of a human ship. There were broken barrels scattered on the ground. Some sunlight filtered down from above.

Coral ignored all of that. She swam right to a half-open chest that was lit by a single sunbeam. "Over here!" she shouted.

"Wow!" Angel gasped. "Look at all these coins!"

Coral picked one up. "They're beautiful!" Purrmaids sometimes found one or
two human coins around the ocean. But
the girls had never seen this many in one
place. "I'm going to bring a gold coin to
school tomorrow!" she announced.

"That's a great idea!" Angel said.

Coral's cheeks hurt
from grinning. *I'm so
glad I was brave!* she
thought. She squeezed
the coin in her paw and
said, "Let's get back
to the South Canary
Current. It's time to go
home!"

The girls closed the lid of the chest and
turned around to leave. Suddenly, the sunlight disappeared. "What happened to the
sun?" Shelly asked.

Coral looked up. There was nothing blocking the holes in the deck. "It must have gotten cloudy," she answered.

"It's really dark now," Angel said. "I can't even see my tail!"

Coral scanned the darkened water. She pointed to a brighter spot in the darkness. "I think that's the hole we used to get down here. Let's head that way and see if we can get out."

The purrmaids dodged corals and sea sponges as they swam slowly toward the light. But Coral realized they weren't swimming toward sunlight. Sunlight wasn't green, and this light definitely was. This was more of a glow than a ray of light.

There were many harmless creatures in the ocean that glowed. Sea pens, krill, and lantern fish could all glow. Coral didn't think this was any of those things. None of them had sharp, scary teeth. But this thing did!

Coral hissed. "Quick! Hide!" She grabbed her friends' paws and pulled them behind a barrel. When they were hidden, she carefully peeked out to get a better look at the glowing creature.

The eerie green glow circled around the hold. It paused near the barrel. Now it was close enough for Coral to see its eyes.

"It looks like a monster!" Shelly whispered.

Coral bit her lip. "I think it's a shark," she said.

"A shark!" Angel gasped. "I knew we should have just gone home!"

Coral scowled. Angel was probably right. But they couldn't change that now. They had to think of some way to escape.

The trio huddled together. "The next time he moves away," Coral said, "we should swim as fast as we can!"

Shelly and Angel nodded. They watched the ghostly glow pass back and forth through the murky waters. Then it began to head toward the barrel. "What is he doing?" Angel gasped.

Coral panicked. *This is all my fault,* she thought. *We never should have come down to the hold.*

The shark paused at a giant sea fan. The glow from his skin cast creepy shadows on the ocean floor. That's when Coral saw her chance.

"Go, go, go!" she hissed.

Angel and Shelly raced away. Coral didn't follow them.

She knew they couldn't all outswim the shark. To make sure her friends were safe, Coral had to create a distraction.

She knew what she had to do.

Coral squared her shoulders. She popped up from behind the barrel and swam straight at the shark. When she got close, she tucked her head down and threw her tail back. Hopefully, the bubbles from her underwater flip would get the shark's attention.

It worked. He tilted his head toward her.

Shelly and Angel had reached a hole in the hold's wall. They just needed a little more time to get to safety. So Coral let go of her coin and waved her paws around while shouting, "Over here, Mr. Shark! Eat me if you want! But stay away from my friends!"

The green-glowing shark swam slowly in Coral's direction. She felt herself trembling.

But she had to be strong. She forced herself to look directly at the shark.

When they were eye to eye, though, Coral's courage faded away. She gulped.

The shark said, "Eat you? Why would I want to eat you?"

8

"You're—you're not here to eat me?" Coral stammered.

"Of course not!" the shark snapped.

"But you're a shark. That's what you do." Coral scratched her head. "Isn't it?"

"Catsharks always get a bad rap," he grumbled. "Everyone in the ocean thinks we're out to eat them!" He gestured at a stack of pale yellow pouches that hung from the sea fan. "I'm stuck here baby-sitting. These are my cousins. My mom and my aunt went to get a bite to eat."

Coral's eyes grew wide. The shark saw that she was scared, so he shouted, "Worms! We eat worms! Or tiny fish! Or shrimp!"

Coral exhaled with relief. "I didn't know you weren't a purrmaid-eating type of shark," she admitted.

"Well, you're not the only one." The shark sighed. "Why do you think we live inside a shipwreck? Nobody wants us around. Everyone says we're too danger-ous." He swam back to the sea fan. "No one even bothers to get to know us."

Coral felt awful. She didn't know anything about catsharks.

She swam to his side. "I'm Coral," she said. "I'm a purrmaid from Kittentail Cove."

"I'm Chomp," he answered. "I'm from right here."

Coral giggled. "It's nice to meet you, Chomp."

"What are you doing down here inside the shipwreck?" Chomp asked. "And the two purrmaids who swam away—were those your friends?"

Coral nodded. "My best friends, actually. We were trying to find the South Canary Current. Then we saw the shipwreck, and we wanted to explore."

"It's a pretty cool place to live," Chomp said.

"It really is!" Coral agreed. "But it's time for us to get home."

"Come and visit again sometime," Chomp said.

"And you should come visit me, too!" Coral suggested. "All you have to do is ride the South Canary Current. It will bring you directly to the entrance of Kittentail Cove."

"I'll remember that!" Chomp answered. He waved goodbye.

By the time Coral swam out of the shipwreck, she was grinning from ear to ear. It had been an exciting day!

Then Angel's voice startled her. "Coral! You're alive!"

Shelly and Angel hurried over to their friend's side. "We thought you were right behind us,"

Shelly said. "When we got out and you weren't here . . . we didn't know what to do!"

"We were so scared!" Angel added.

"I didn't mean to scare you," Coral said. "I wanted to give you more time to get away. But I didn't need to do that!"

"What happened with the monster?" Shelly asked.

"He isn't a monster!" Coral explained.

"He's a catshark, and catsharks don't eat purrmaids."

"What a relief!" Shelly said.

"I think there's been enough adventure today," Angel purred. "Let's get to the current so we can go home."

The purrmaids hurried up to the South Canary Current. It was as crowded as Angel's mother had warned it would be.

From time to time, they got bumped by turtles, fish, and even other purrmaids. The girls stayed close together and kept an eye on each other.

When they took the exit to Kittentail Cove and swam through the gates of the town, Coral glanced up at the clock tower. "We made it!" she cried. "It isn't dinnertime yet!"

"That means we won't get grounded," Angel laughed, "*and* we found the coolest treasures to bring to school tomorrow!"

Coral froze. Her gold coin! "Oh no!" she moaned. "I don't have my treasure!"

"What do you mean?" Shelly asked.

"I must have dropped my coin at the shipwreck!" Coral said. "When I was trying to get Chomp's attention, I started waving my paws around." She looked down at her tail. "I think I let go of it then."

Angel and Shelly glanced at each other.

"You can have my treasure," Shelly offered.

"Or mine," Angel added.

Coral shook her head. "It's really nice of you to say that," she said. "But I can't take your stuff! That wouldn't be fair." She sighed. "It's my fault I lost the coin. I'll just bring in that shell from my collection."

Coral tried to cheer up as they swam home. But when they reached Leondra's Square, she was still feeling down. Her friends each gave her a hug when they said goodbye, but even that didn't help.

"We'll see you here tomorrow?" Angel asked.

Coral nodded. "Of course."

"Smile, Coral," Shelly said. "Things will be better tomorrow, I'm sure."

Coral tried to smile for Shelly. But in her heart, she was thinking, *They couldn't get any worse.*

Coral hardly slept that night. She tossed and turned on her oyster-shell bed for hours.

She knew she was running behind because she was moving so slowly. But when she got to Leondra's Square to meet up with Angel and Shelly, she realized how late she was. Not only was Shelly already waiting, but Angel was there, too!

"Sorry I'm a little slow today," Coral said.

"Don't worry!" Angel answered. Shelly and Angel exchanged a glance. They had huge grins on their faces.

"Let's get to school," Shelly suggested. "We have our treasures now!"

Coral bit her lip. It was nice to see Angel and Shelly so excited about the treasures they found in the shipwreck. It wasn't their fault that Coral had lost hers. She forced herself to smile and swam alongside her friends.

As the students arrived in Eel-Twelve, Ms. Harbor welcomed them. "I hope you all brought something to share," she said. The students nodded. Ms. Harbor smiled. "I can't wait to see your treasures and begin getting to know all of you."

"Can I go first?" Baker asked.

"No, me!" Taylor shouted.

"Everyone will get a turn, I purr-omise," Ms. Harbor said.

Ms. Harbor called up one purrmaid at a time to present a treasure. Coral did her best to pay attention, but she kept thinking about the gold coin. *I can't believe I lost it,* she thought. *It would have been so purr-fect for today!*

Coral didn't notice it was Angel's turn until Shelly tapped her shoulder. She looked up and saw that Angel was floating in the front of the classroom.

"Shelly and I will present together," Angel announced. She winked at Coral.

Of course they're presenting as a team, Coral thought. *The spyglass and compass go together.*

Shelly tugged on Coral's paw. "Come on, Coral," she said.

Coral shook her head. "I don't have my

coin," she whispered. "My treasure doesn't match yours!"

"You're wrong!" Shelly said. She dragged Coral to float next to Angel.

"There are many things in the ocean that are special to Shelly and me," Angel said. "But nothing is more special than family and friends."

"We're both really lucky to have fintastic families," Shelly continued. "But the treasure Angel and I want to share today is our best friend, Coral."

All eyes turned to Coral. She didn't understand what was going on. Angel didn't give her a chance to ask any questions. "Yesterday, we learned that the most special things in the world are the ones we hold close to our hearts," Angel said.

"Sometimes Coral can be extra careful," Shelly continued, "and that can make some purrmaids think she's a scaredy cat."

"But she's not!" Angel said. "She's actually one of the bravest purrmaids I know."

"She's only cautious because she cares so much about her friends," Shelly added. "Coral would do anything for us, and we would do anything for her."

"There is nothing closer to our hearts

than our best friend," Angel said.

"What a wonderful presentation!" Ms. Harbor cried. "Well done, Shelly and Angel!"

Coral could feel her face getting hot. "I treasure you two, as well," she said, and the whole class cheered.

10

Coral was very quiet as she swam out to recess. She was speechless after Shelly and Angel's presentation. They had made her feel so loved and special. She couldn't believe how lucky she was to have such good friends.

Angel and Shelly weren't sure why Coral was so quiet. "Did we do something wrong?" Shelly asked.

"We were trying to be nice," Angel added.

"No, no, no!" Coral cried. She rushed forward to hug her friends. "That was one of the nicest things anyone has ever done for me!"

Shelly and Angel beamed. But the moment was interrupted when the girls heard their classmate Taylor scream, "A shark!"

"He's coming for us!" Baker shouted. "Swim for your lives!"

Coral whipped around to see what was happening. That's when she saw someone familiar.

The other purrmaids cowered behind the rock benches in the schoolyard. Ms. Harbor swam toward the shark, ready to protect her students. Coral darted forward and put herself between the shark and Ms. Harbor. "Chomp!" she shouted. "What are you doing here?"

Chomp grinned, and all of his teeth were on display. That caused a new chorus of screams from Coral's classmates.

"Get away, Coral! He'll eat you!" Taylor yelled.

Coral turned around and shook her head. "No, he won't," she replied. She motioned for the purrmaids to stop hiding. Angel and Shelly gulped, but they swam out from behind the benches. The rest of her classmates poked their heads out but didn't come forward.

Coral said, "Ms. Harbor, I'd like to introduce you to someone—my new friend, Chomp."

Ms. Harbor opened and closed her mouth like a fish. But she didn't make a sound. Chomp gave her a toothy grin and extended his fin. Coral nodded at her teacher. Ms. Harbor finally put her paw out so they could shake.

"Chomp is a catshark," Coral continued, "and yesterday, I learned a lot." She winked at Shelly and Angel. "My best friends helped me learn that I don't have to be a scaredy cat about new things." She smiled at Chomp. "And Chomp taught me that catsharks aren't dangerous. They are just misunderstood."

"Really?" Baker asked.

"Really," Chomp answered. "I didn't come to Kittentail Cove for lunch! I came to give this to Coral." He held out a small package wrapped in seaweed.

"What is that?" Ms. Harbor asked.

Chomp grinned again. "Coral isn't the only one who learned something," he explained. "She taught me there are other good fish in the sea. You just have to be willing to give them a chance, and maybe you'll make a new friend."

Coral unwrapped the package. Inside were three gold coins from the shipwreck!

"After you left," Chomp said, "I realized you dropped your coin. I wanted to bring it to you so you'd always remember me." He giggled. "I brought some extras—for your two friends. And I added some hooks so you can attach them to your bracelets. That way you won't lose them!"

Once again, Coral was speechless.

"How fin-tastic!" Ms. Harbor cheered. "Thank you both for teaching us about catsharks. And thank you for visiting, Chomp, and for introducing him, Coral. What a purr-fect thing to share with the class—a new friend!"

The entire class cheered. Coral gave Chomp a big hug. The other purrmaids swam up to him and started asking questions. Coral pulled Angel and Shelly aside. She held out a gold coin to each of them.

"But Chomp gave those to you!" Angel said.

Coral shook her head. "He wanted us each to have a coin. We can put them on our bracelets to remind us to be brave."

"That is a paw-some plan!" Shelly cried.

Coral put her gold coin on her bracelet.
She smiled and purred, "I can't wait for our
next adventure!"

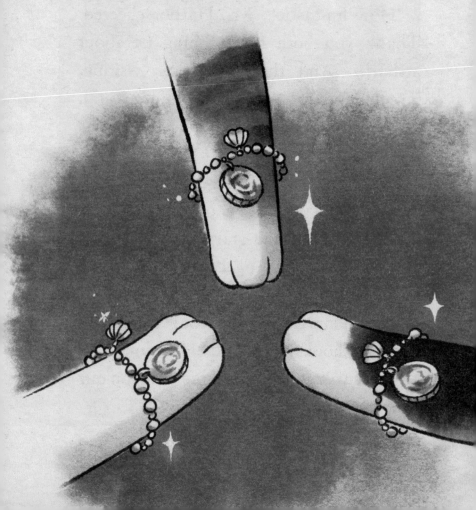

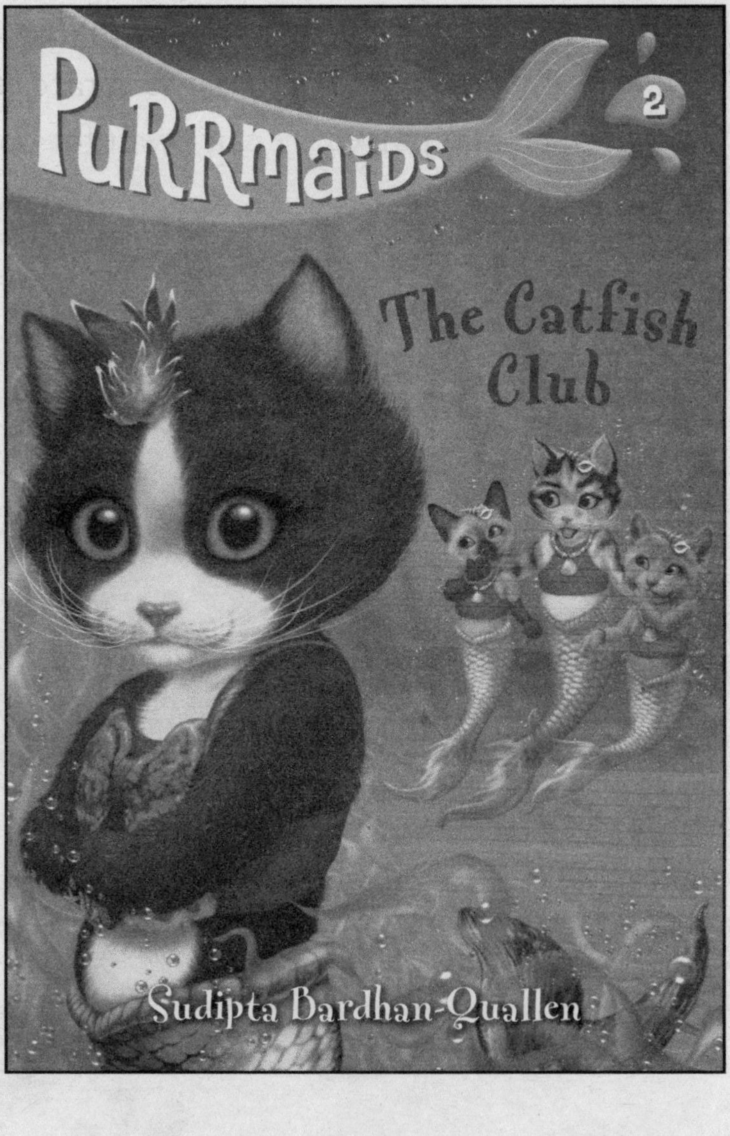
PuRRmaiDs
2
The Catfish Club
Sudipta Bardhan-Quallen

To my favorite artist, Brooklyn Quallen

Angel loved almost everything about living in Kittentail Cove. The one thing she definitely did not love was getting ready in the morning.

"Angel," Mommy purred, "you have to get out of bed!"

"But it's so early!" Angel yowled. She covered her eyes with her paws. "Just a little bit longer?"

Mommy pulled off her daughter's seaweed blanket. "If you don't get up now, you'll be late meeting Coral and Shelly. You don't want to swim to sea school alone, do you?" she asked.

Angel pushed some fur out of her eyes and scowled. Mommy was right. She couldn't be late to see her best friends, Coral and Shelly. She loved exploring Kittentail Cove with them!

Angel was as bold as her black-and-white fur made her look. She was creative and daring, and loved making a splash. Shelly was a purrmaid with silky white fur, which she liked to keep purr-fectly clean. And orange kitten Coral could sometimes be a scaredy cat, which is why Angel loved helping her be brave!

As far back as Angel could remember, she had been friends with Shelly and Coral. It was hard to believe that three kittens who were so different inside and out could be such a good team. But they were! And Angel felt lucky to have two fin-tastic friends.

All three purrmaids were in the same class at sea school this year, and their teacher, Ms. Harbor, was paw-some.

Thinking of sea school made Angel smile. She twirled out of her oyster-shell bed. She stretched her paws up and her tail down.

She pulled on her new red top. Finally, she turned to the jewelry box on the table next to the bed.

Angel opened the lid and picked up her favorite bracelet. It had two beautiful charms on it—a golden seashell and a gold coin. Coral and Shelly had matching bracelets. They got the seashell charms to celebrate their friendship. They added the gold coins after they met Chomp the catshark in a ship-wreck. Both charms reminded Angel of the fun adventures she'd had with her friends.

Her bracelet looked great, but Angel wanted more today. She put on a necklace made of angel wing shells. Then she grabbed the lavender pearl earrings that Mommy had given her on her birthday. She loved them. No one else she knew had earrings like that.

"Angel!" Mommy shouted. "Come and eat breakfast."

Angel rushed to the kitchen. Mommy held out a plate of seaweed pancakes and fish eggs. "My favorite!" Angel purred.

"Anything for my best kitten," Mommy replied. "Are you girls still coming to my office after sea school today?"

Angel nodded. "Shelly and Coral are really excited," she said. Mommy was on the Kittentail Cove Council. Her office was in Cove Council Hall. There was always something happening there. Today there was an extra treat for Angel and her friends. The council was getting a special tour of the Kittentail Cove Museum. Mommy was bringing Angel, Shelly, and Coral to the tour as her guests. Angel couldn't wait!

"See you this afternoon!" Angel said, kissing Mommy goodbye.

She swam to Leondra's Square and spotted flashes of white fur next to orange fur.

Coral and Shelly were already waiting for her.

"Angel!" Coral shouted. "We're going to be late!"

Angel giggled. Coral was always thinking about following the rules and not getting into trouble. "You don't have to worry about being late when you can swim fast!" she shouted. "I bet I can get there first!"

When the girls arrived at sea school, they hurried to room Eel-Twelve. As they swam through the classroom door, they saw the walls covered in posters. Each poster showed a different work of art from the Kittentail Cove Museum. "Wow!" Shelly purred.

"Do you like them?" Ms. Harbor asked.

Angel looked at her friends. "We love them!" she said.

"Wonderful!" Ms. Harbor said. "Then you will enjoy our art lesson today."

Angel grinned. Shelly loved cooking. Coral loved reading. But art was Angel's specialty! "This one was painted by Clawed Monet, right?" she asked, pointing. "And this is a Jackson Pawlock!"

"Slow down!" Ms. Harbor laughed. "Don't give away my lesson."

The bell rang, and the class took their seats. Ms. Harbor raised a paw. "Good morning, everyone," she said. "Today we are going to talk about art. We can learn a lot about purrmaid history from studying great artists and their masterpieces." She swam to one of the posters. "This is a painting by Pablo Picatso." She moved to the next one. "And this is a sculpture by Henri Catisse."

Someone behind Angel whispered, "I could do that." Angel looked over her shoulder to see who it was. It was a purrmaid named Adrianna.

The two girls sitting next to Adrianna giggled. Their names were Umiko and Cascade. Angel didn't know the other girls very well, but she knew that they were usually together doing the same things. They called themselves the Catfish Club.

Angel frowned. She didn't like anyone interrupting her teacher.

Umiko saw Angel's face and shushed her friends. The Catfish Club quieted down, and Angel was able to turn back to the lesson.

"Who knows why this artwork is special?" Ms. Harbor asked. When no one answered, she explained, "The artists didn't worry about what others told them to do. They didn't follow the rules. They followed their hearts! Their work helps the rest of us see the beauty in our world. Pay attention to what you like! For homework, I want you to work in groups to create your own masterpieces," she announced.

2

The class purred with excitement as soon as Ms. Harbor made her announcement.

Angel leaned toward Shelly and Coral. "We're all working together, right?" Angel whispered.

"Of course!" Coral laughed.

"I wouldn't want to work with anyone but you two," Shelly added.

Some students had questions. "Ms. Harbor, how are we supposed to do this homework?" Baker asked. "We're not real artists."

"And where are we supposed to get supplies?" Taylor added. He looked worried.

Ms. Harbor grinned. "First of all," she said, "each of you is *absolutely* a real artist! Whatever you create from your heart is real art. You don't need fish oil paint or squid ink brushes to make art! There are beautiful things all around us." She pointed to the ocean outside the classroom window. "Anything can be art."

The purrmaids in the class slowly nodded. Baker and Taylor looked more relaxed. But Angel wasn't feeling relaxed. She wasn't feeling worried, either. Angel was excited! "This is the best homework ever!" she whispered.

Normally, when Angel was that excited, it was hard for her to sit still and listen. But not while Ms. Harbor talked about all her favorite artists! When the bell rang, she was disappointed that the day was over!

Right after school, the girls headed to Cove Council Hall. Shelly and Coral struggled to keep up with Angel.

"Slow down, Angel!" Coral begged.

"Why are you speeding?" Shelly panted.

"The tour!" Angel replied. "I want to be the first ones to see the museum after the grand makeover!"

Everyone knew Angel loved being first. Winning, getting prizes, and being the best were all things that Angel tried hard to do. But going to the museum today wasn't just about winning. She thought they could brainstorm some good ideas for their homework from the museum.

Angel practically dragged Mommy out of her office. But when the four of them reached the front door of the museum, it was locked! Mommy looked at her watch. "The tour doesn't start for fifteen minutes," she explained. "We will have to wait."

"Rats!" Angel grumbled. All she wanted to do was to go inside.

"Let's get in line," Shelly suggested, "so we can be the first ones in."

"Great idea!" Angel agreed.

The girls lined up right in front of the museum. Slowly, other purrmaids gathered around the door, too. But the tour couldn't start without Mayor Rivers. "Where is the mayor?" Angel wondered, straining to see over the crowd of purrmaids.

Finally, she spied him. "We're going to be able to go in soon!" Angel squealed. She grabbed her friends' paws and danced around with happiness.

Mayor Rivers stopped near Mommy, and Angel's heart sank. He always talked for so long! Now they would have to wait again.

As she frowned at the talkative mayor, Angel didn't notice anyone swimming past. But then Shelly yowled, "Hey! You can't cut in front of us!"

It was the Catfish Club!

The three purrmaids didn't look alike. Adrianna's fur was silky and gray. Umiko's fur was white with orange and black patches. And Cascade's fur was a short cinnamon brown. But there was something about them that made them look like triplets.

After scowling for a moment, Angel realized what made the Catfish Club look so much alike. Each girl was wearing lavender. Their clothes were lavender. Their earrings were lavender. Their headbands were lavender. Even the pearl necklaces they wore were made from lavender pearls.

Lots of purrmaids had pearl jewelry. After all, they lived under the sea! But most pearls were white or black. Lavender pearls were very rare. That's what made Angel's earrings so special. She touched one of her earrings and thought, *There's no way three purrmaids would be wearing that much lavender on the same day without planning it ahead of time.*

Coral said, "You three need to get to the back of the line."

Umiko shrugged and started to swim away. But Adrianna grabbed her paw to stop her. "Was there a line?" she asked. She sounded innocent, but there was something fishy about the way she smiled.

Angel felt her face growing hot. She hissed, "Of course there was a line!"

"Actually," Cascade added, "this isn't a *line*. It's a crowd. So we can't really get to the back of the line."

Adrianna crossed her paws. "Besides," she shouted, "we're not going anywhere just because *you* tell us to!"

3

"My uncle is the mayor," Adrianna said, "and he said we could wait at the museum door."

"It doesn't matter what your uncle says!" Angel replied. "You have to wait your turn!"

Angel and Adrianna glared at each other. Coral and Shelly swam over and hovered next to Angel. They wanted to show the Catfish Club that they were on Angel's side. Cascade and Umiko did the same with

Adrianna. The two groups of girls stared each other down.

Angel was so mad she wanted to scream.

Mayor Rivers interrupted the staring contest. "Is there a problem?" he asked. Mommy swam behind him to see what was going on.

Angel went to Mommy's side. "Those three," she said, pointing at the Catfish Club, "cut in front of us."

Adrianna shook her head. "Uncle Ray," she said to Mayor Rivers, "we didn't know there was a line! We're just excited about the tour."

"I'm sure my niece and her friends didn't mean to cause trouble," Mayor Rivers said.

"We just want to be first," Umiko added.

The Catfish Club looked down at their tails like they were embarrassed. But Angel didn't believe it. "Well, we were here before you," she snapped. "And I like being first, too."

Angel tried to swim toward the other girls, but Mommy held her back. "It doesn't matter who is at the front of the line," Mommy purred. "We'll all be able to enjoy the artwork. Don't you agree, Angel?"

"Just let them go in," Shelly whispered into Angel's ear.

"We could get in trouble if we keep fighting!" Coral added. "We don't need to be first."

Angel didn't *need* to be first. But she enjoyed it. Just like she enjoyed winning and being the best. She really wanted to push those purrmaids out of line, but she knew her mother and her friends were right. Acting like the Catfish Club would make her just as bad as they were. She didn't like it, but she nodded anyway.

Luckily, Mrs. Clearwater, the director of the museum, opened the door. "Welcome to our special tour of Kittentail Cove Museum," she said. She steered everyone inside. Soon small groups of purrmaids swam off to explore the museum.

The Catfish Club went to the east wing of the museum. So Coral said, "We should go to the west wing!"

Angel stopped to look at a giant clam-shell. The inside of the shell was splattered with different colors of fish oil paint. "It's the Jackson Pawlock painting from Ms. Harbor's poster!" she exclaimed.

Shelly tilted her head and squinted at the shell. "It's purr-ty," she said, "but he must have made a whale of a mess."

Angel giggled. Shelly hated to get her paws dirty! "Should we do something like this for our homework?" she teased.

Shelly shook her head and groaned.

Coral was on the other side of the gal-lery. She waved for her friends to come over. "Look at this one!" she shouted.

Coral hovered in front of a large canvas made from a sail from a shipwreck. It was a beautiful night scene of a town that looked a lot like Kittentail Cove. The moon and stars shone through the ocean and lit up the night sky.

"It's beautiful," Angel purred.

"Yes, it is," Mrs. Clearwater agreed. Angel turned around. The museum director was swimming beside Mommy. "It's one of my favorites," she continued. "Did you see what Vincent Fang Gogh used in this picture?"

Angel swam closer to the canvas. "It's not just paint," she gasped. "I see pearls and sea glass, too!"

Mrs. Clearwater nodded. "Exactly! Fang Gogh searched the ocean for things that would look like little strokes and spots of color. Up close, all you see are the spots. But swim away a bit," she explained, "and the spots come together to make a stunning starry night!"

"He was so creative!" Shelly said. "I never would have used pearls and sea glass."

"I thought you could only use paint," Coral added.

Mrs. Clearwater grinned. "Fang Gogh shows us how things that are lovely on their own can come together and create something even more special."

Mommy looked from Angel to Coral

to Shelly. "Just like the three of you are paw-some by yourselves, but when you get together, you're paw-sitively amazing!"

Angel gave Mommy a hug. She was right! Angel was smarter, braver, cooler, and more paw-some when Coral and Shelly were around!

Suddenly, Angel had an idea. "Mrs. Clearwater," she said, "we're supposed to create a piece of artwork for our homework tonight. Could we work on it here?"

"That's a great idea," Mommy agreed.

Mrs. Clearwater grinned. "Of course!"

The purrmaids followed Mrs. Clearwater through the halls of the museum. "I'll take you girls to the storage room," she said. "You can get inspiration from all the masterpieces that aren't on display right now. And there are lots of interesting things that you can use."

They swam past all the exhibits and soon reached a set of heavy double doors. The girls helped Mrs. Clearwater prop them open.

"Here you go," Mrs. Clearwater said. "You can work with anything you find in here!"

Angel smiled and led her friends inside. But what she saw made her freeze in place. "What is the Catfish Club doing here?" she sputtered.

4

"Do you girls know each other?" Mrs. Clearwater asked.

Angel rolled her eyes and muttered, "Unfortunately."

Coral nodded. "We're in the same class, Mrs. Clearwater," she answered.

"That's why you have the same homework!" Mrs. Clearwater said. "Have fun working together. Let me know if you need anything else."

As soon as Mrs. Clearwater was gone, Adrianna hissed, "You're being copycats."

"You heard us ask Mrs. Clearwater if we could work on our art project," Cascade added, "so you did, too?"

"Of course we didn't!" Coral exclaimed. "We didn't know you were going to be here. Angel had this idea all on her own."

The Catfish Club girls didn't look convinced.

"We were here first," Umiko said. "Maybe you guys should leave."

"We're not leaving!" Shelly yowled.

Angel sighed. She wanted to do their homework, not fight with the Catfish Club. "Maybe we should start over?" she suggested. "We're all in Ms. Harbor's class. We should at least try to be friends."

Umiko and Cascade nodded, but Adrianna crossed her paws. "You guys have been mean to us all afternoon," she said. "Why would we want to be friends?"

"Mean? Us?" Angel gasped. *They* were the ones who cut the line. *They* were the ones who were rude. *They* were the problem! "Oh, just forget it," she said. "You work on your project. We'll work on ours."

The Catfish Club began to swim away. Umiko stopped and looked back at Angel, Coral, and Shelly. "Let's try to stay out of each other's way," she suggested.

After Umiko left, Coral said, "I think she's right about steering clear of each other. I don't want to get into any trouble."

Angel led her friends in the opposite direction. They began searching for materials for their art project.

The museum's storage room was fintastic. Angel had never seen anything like it. It was as big as a blue whale! There were aisles of shelves that stretched back as far as she could see. "There's a lot here to explore!" she said.

"Look at this!" Coral shouted. She pointed to a row of statues on a high shelf. She swam next to one of a purrmaid perched on the edge of a rock, resting her chin on her paw. Coral copied the statue's pose. "Guess what I'm thinking!"

"I hope you're think-ing about our project!" Angel giggled.

Shelly joined in on the fun. She struck a pose with her chin up and her paws clasped behind her back. "Who am I?" she asked.

"The Kitten Dancer!" Angel cried. She swam to

the original statue on the lowest shelf. "One of my favorites!"

Angel could have spent the entire afternoon looking at all the statues, but that wasn't going to help with their homework! "Maybe we can come back to these if we finish our project," she said.

Shelly and Coral nodded. The girls moved to another set of shelves. This one didn't hold statues. Instead, there were large pieces of driftwood covered in bright, bold shapes.

"Do you know who painted these?" Coral asked.

Angel grinned. "Pablo Picatso!" she answered. "Remember how Ms. Harbor told us that anything can be art?" She pointed to some paintings. "Picatso used rectangles, circles, and zigzags to create these portraits."

"You know so much about art," Shelly said. "We're lucky to be working with you."

"Thank you!" Angel purred.

"I really like this," Coral said. She pointed to a painting of a purrmaid looking at her reflection in a mirror. "Do you think we should paint a portrait of Ms. Harbor?"

Angel's eyes lit up. "That is a paw-some idea!"

The purrmaids split up to find the supplies they needed. Coral found a bag filled with fish oil paints. Shelly picked up sea sponges, sea pens, and soft coral brushes.

But they needed something to paint on.

Angel scanned the aisles of the storage room, looking for something they could use as a canvas. She spied a giant sheet of seaweed paper. It was purr-fect! And it was big enough for two paintings in case they made a mistake.

Angel swam toward the paper. But just as she was about to reach for it, someone else's paws appeared. "This is paw-some!" a voice called out.

It was the Catfish Club, taking *her* paper!

5

Angel returned to her friends empty-handed. "I found a great piece of seaweed paper to use for our portrait," she explained, "but Adrianna got it before I did." She hung her head.

"Don't worry, Angel," Shelly said. "There have to be other things that would work."

Angel nodded, even though she was still upset.

The three purrmaids searched for something else to use for their project. "How about that?" Coral asked, pointing at a flat rock.

Angel shook her head. "It's too heavy," she said. "We'd need more paws to help carry it out of the museum."

"You're right," Coral agreed.

They went back to their search. But instead of finding something lighter, the purrmaids found the Catfish Club. They seemed to be on the hunt for something, too.

"I wonder what they're looking for," Angel whispered.

Shelly and Coral shrugged. "I don't know," Shelly said, "but maybe we should go the other way."

They tried to turn around quietly and swim away before they were seen, but it wasn't their lucky day. Adrianna spotted them and shouted, "Hey! Are you spying on us?"

Angel spun around to face the Catfish Club. "Of course not," she snapped. "We're looking for something to paint a portrait on."

"We already found this," Adrianna said, holding up the seaweed paper.

"But we haven't found any paints," Umiko added.

"Or brushes," Cascade said. "Not even a sea sponge!"

"We found paint," Coral said, "and a whole bunch of sponges and brushes."

Adrianna's eyes narrowed. "Did you three take all the supplies?" she asked. "I'm telling! Wait until my uncle the mayor hears about this!"

"We took what we found," Shelly replied, "like Mrs. Clearwater said we could."

"You didn't leave brushes for anyone else to use," Umiko said.

"And you three didn't leave seaweed paper for us, either," Angel snapped.

"Well, what are we supposed to do now?" Cascade asked.

Angel glanced at Shelly and Coral. She had an idea. She just couldn't believe what she was about to say.

Angel pulled her friends toward her. She wanted to talk to them without the other girls hearing. "We can't do our project without paper," she whispered. "And they can't do their project without paints and tools. We're all stuck, unless . . ." She paused and bit her lip.

Shelly finished Angel's sentence. "Unless we share."

Coral agreed. "I think that makes sense," she said. "I don't want to get in trouble if we don't finish our homework."

"So it's decided?" Angel asked.

Her friends nodded.

Angel held the fish oil paint and brushes out to the Catfish Club. "If you guys will share your seaweed paper," she said, "then we'll share our supplies."

"I thought of that already," Cascade purred. "I was going to suggest it, too. It's the best plan."

"I vote yes," Umiko added.

After a moment, Adrianna shrugged. "I guess we can do that," she agreed.

The girls split up the supplies, and then carefully cut the seaweed paper in half. Soon each group had everything they needed.

"I can't wait to actually *start* on this project!" Angel exclaimed.

Then she overheard the Catfish Club's conversation. Umiko said, "Let's go, girls. We can finally get to work!"

"It's going to be so paw-some," Cascade said.

"The best in the whole class," Adrianna added.

Angel couldn't hold back. "The best in the class?" she snorted.

"Ignore them," Coral whispered. "It's not a contest." She tried to pull her friend away.

Angel frowned. Coral was right. It really wasn't a contest. But even when no one else was competing, Angel hated to lose! "I bet it won't be the best," she shouted.

"What?" Umiko asked.

"I said," Angel answered, "I bet your project won't be the best in the class."

"Really?" Cascade asked. "What would you bet?"

Angel paused for a moment. She knew she was getting too upset, but she couldn't help herself. She yelled, "I would bet *anything* that Ms. Harbor likes what we make more than whatever you three come up with!"

Adrianna's eyes narrowed. "Would you

bet those earrings?" she hissed.

Angel's paw went right to one of her pearls. "What?" she yelped.

Umiko swam between Adrianna and Angel. "Let's stop this," she said. "Someone is going to say something she doesn't mean—"

But Adrianna cut Umiko off. "You said you'd bet anything," she said to Angel. "We want to bet your earrings."

Angel didn't want to risk losing her lavender pearl earrings. Her friends knew it, too. Shelly whispered, "Angel, you love those earrings. This bet isn't worth it."

"Let's just go," Coral suggested.

Angel was about to nod when Adrianna said, "We get it. You're just a chicken in the sea."

"Actually," Cascade whispered, "chickens don't live in the ocean. So she couldn't really be a chicken in the sea."

Adrianna elbowed Cascade to be quiet. Coral and Shelly tried to hide their mouths with their paws so no one would see them giggling. But Angel didn't pay attention to Cascade's funny fact. She clenched her jaw so much that it hurt. Then she shouted, "You want to make a bet? Fine! What are you going to give us when our project is better than yours?"

That made the Catfish Club quiet down. They looked at each other. Then Cascade said, "Your earrings match our necklaces, so if Ms. Harbor likes your art better, we'll give you one. But if she likes what we make more, then you give us your earrings."

Angel ignored the looks on her friends' faces and declared, "It's a bet. May the best artists win!"

6

Shelly and Coral yanked Angel away from the Catfish Club almost immediately.

"What did you do, Angel?" Coral cried. "You can't give them your earrings!"

"What would your mother say if you lost them?" Shelly added. "It would be a cat-tastrophe!"

"You would get in so much trouble!" Coral gasped. "In fact, you might even get *us* in trouble!"

"Relax!" Angel replied. "There's no way they can do a better job than we can."

Coral and Shelly shook their heads. "We hope you're right, Angel," Coral said.

Angel waved her friends over to a table in a corner of the storage room. "Let's get to work," she said. They cleared the table off, and Angel carefully unrolled the seaweed paper. Shelly found an oyster-shell palette and carefully squeezed different colors of paint onto it. Coral arranged the brushes and sponges on the table.

"How should we start?" Shelly asked.

Coral shrugged. "I've never painted a portrait before," she admitted, "or used fish oil paint."

Angel hadn't, either. But how hard could it be? She picked up a sponge and dunked it in some green paint. "I guess we can start with the background," she suggested. She started to swab the paint across the paper.

"That looks great!" Shelly commented.

Angel smiled. "Thanks!" She put the sponge down and dipped a brush in black paint. She started to paint a circle for Ms. Harbor's face. But when Angel pulled the brush along the seaweed paper, something terrible happened. "Rats!" she yelped.

"What is it?" Coral asked.

Angel moved the brush aside and pointed. "The paper ripped!" she cried.

Coral and Shelly examined the tear. "It isn't so bad," Shelly said. She softly pushed the edges of the paper down. "Let's just be more careful."

"I was being gentle, I promise!" Angel said.

"We know, Angel," Coral soothed.

Angel held the brush out to Shelly and Coral. "Maybe one of you should try," she suggested. "I don't want to make it worse."

Shelly picked up the brush and dipped it into the paint. Then she lightly brushed it against the seaweed paper. She finished the circle.

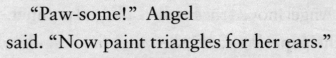

"Paw-some!" Angel said. "Now paint triangles for her ears."

Shelly nodded and turned to the paper again. She carefully painted one ear. But when she lifted the brush off to get more paint, a chunk of the paper stuck to it and tore off!

"I'm sorry!" Shelly yowled. Before, there was just a little tear in the seaweed paper. Now there was a hole where Ms. Harbor's ear should be.

"It isn't your fault," Coral said. She put a paw around Shelly's shoulders. "The same thing happened to Angel."

Angel nodded. "Coral is right. I guess we just don't know how to work with seaweed paper and fish oil paint."

"Maybe we could cut off a smaller piece and start over?" Coral suggested.

Angel shook her head. "I think the paper is too thin," she said. "It wasn't the best idea to try to paint on it. Especially since we've never done it before."

"What are we going to do now?" Shelly asked. "You need a project that can win your bet with the Catfish Club."

Angel bit her lip. *I wish I hadn't lost my temper and made that bet,* she thought. There was no way Ms. Harbor would think a portrait filled with rips and tears was the better project. She felt butterfly fish fluttering in her tummy.

"Should we search for more supplies?" Coral wondered. "There has to be something here we know how to use."

"I guess," Angel said. "We don't really have a choice. And we can look for a trash can, too." She crumpled up the seaweed paper. "This is just garbage now."

The girls nodded sadly. They began

to swim down the aisles again. They saw many more beautiful pieces of art, but they couldn't find any other art supplies.

Angel spied a trash can at the end of an aisle. "Let's get rid of this," she said, holding up the ball of seaweed paper. Her friends followed her down the aisle.

Before they reached the trash can, Angel heard something. "What's that?" she asked.

Shelly shrugged.

Coral said, "It sounds like someone is upset."

They poked their heads around a corner to see where the noise was coming from.

It was the Catfish Club! They were all crying!

7

Angel squirmed. She didn't like seeing other purrmaids in tears, even when th[ey] got on her nerves. "Should we find [out] what's wrong?" she asked.

"I think that's the right thi[ng,]" Coral said.

Shelly nodded.

The girls slowly app[roached the] Club. Angel tapped [...] and asked, "Are y[ou...]

The Catfish Club flinched at Angel's ...ey ... ...their faces with their ...d out ...ng to do," ...Did you come to ...

...oached the Catfish ...Adrianna's shoulder ...e just worried ...

...asked ...u guys all right?" ...ly behind them. ...r... he...s," she

"We kept ripping holes in the paper," Cascade added, "no matter what we tried."

"And now we don't have an art project at all!" Adrianna cried. She ripped their paper in half over and over until it was just a pile of scraps.

Angel looked down at the crumpled ball in her own paw. They'd all had the same problem. And now they were all in the same mess. No one had homework to bring in tomorrow.

Maybe the Catfish Club isn't so different from us after all, Angel thought. She held out her paw and said, "You guys should know that you didn't do anything wrong."

"Our paper ripped when we tried to paint on it, too," Shelly added.

"I told you seaweed paper is tricky," Cascade sobbed.

The Catfish Club sniffled and glanced at each other. "So you don't have a project, either?" Umiko asked.

Angel, Coral, and Shelly shook their heads. "We're in deep trouble, just like you," Coral said.

"What are you going to do?" Cascade asked. "We don't have any more ideas. *I* can't even think of something!"

"And we don't have a lot of time left," Adrianna added. "Uncle Ray will be taking us home soon."

"We're going to leave soon, too," Shelly said.

The six purrmaids looked down at their tails. Everyone seemed frustrated and a little sad.

Angel remembered how excited she'd been about this homework. *Now it's a cat-tastrophe,* she thought. Her eyes teared up, but she didn't want to cry in front of everyone. So she grabbed the pile of scraps and swam over to the trash can. She lifted the lid to throw away both pieces of ruined seaweed paper.

But when Angel looked inside, her eyes grew wide. "Come here!" she shouted. "Everybody, come here right now!"

"What is it?" Coral asked. She and the others swam swiftly to Angel's side.

Angel pointed to the trash can. "Just look!" she said.

The purrmaids peeked inside. "It's filled with garbage," Adrianna said, confused. "Why are you so excited about trash?"

There was always garbage in Kittentail Cove. Some was created by purrmaids in their daily lives. But there was also rubbish that floated into the cove from human ships and beaches. Keeping their town clean was a way to keep Kittentail Cove purr-ty, but it also

kept sea animals safe. No one in the ocean wanted turtles or seals or birds to accidentally eat a piece of garbage that could harm them.

There were trash cans all over the cove to make it easy to tidy up every last corner. The things that got thrown away looked ugly littering the streets of the town, but that didn't mean they were *always* ugly.

"Anything can be art," Angel said. She grabbed the trash can and dumped the contents on the floor. "We've been thinking about this the wrong way. We don't need fancy paints or papers." She grabbed a metal bottle cap from the pile of garbage. "Look at how shiny this is," she said. "A bunch of these could look like stars shining on a clear ocean night." Then she picked up a handful of sea glass pieces and broken seashells. "And look at how colorful these are. I see all the shades of the buildings of Kittentail Cove."

Umiko reached for a piece of a white plastic wrapper. Humans used things like that to wrap around something they called candy. "This could be cut to look like a moon," she suggested.

"But, Angel," Shelly complained, "it's garbage! It's so dirty!"

"We would make sure everything is clean," Angel explained. She leaned toward Shelly and whispered, "I know you don't like getting dirty."

Shelly smiled at her friend. Then Coral exclaimed, "Angel, you figured it out! We can use these things to make our own *Starry Night* picture!"

Coral and Shelly pulled Angel into a bear hug. "Unless the Catfish Club comes up with a new idea," Coral whispered, "you'll win the bet!"

"Your earrings are safe!" Shelly added.

Out of the corner of her eye, Angel saw the other purrmaids' shoulders slump and their eyes lower. As much as she wanted to win their bet, she knew what she had to do next.

Angel pulled away from her friends and swam toward the Catfish Club. "I think we should—" she began. She paused to take a deep breath before continuing. "I think we should work together."

"All six of us?" Cascade gasped.

Angel nodded. "We're all in the same class. We all want to do a good job." She glanced at the scraps of seaweed paper in the litter pile. "We're all terrible fish oil artists," she joked.

The other girls giggled.

"If we work together," Angel declared, "I know we can create a masterpiece."

8

In an instant, the six purrmaids were smiling and energized. They zipped off in all directions to gather the rest of what they would need.

"I've got snail slime!" Coral shouted. "We can use it as glue."

"We found these," Cascade said. She and Umiko held up a bag of coral pieces.

"I think these are the leftovers from sculpting a coral statue," Umiko said.

"They remind me of the view of Tortoiseshell Reef from Cove Council Hall," Cascade said.

Umiko held up one of the coral pieces. "This one looks a little bit like the statue in Leondra's Square." She giggled.

Angel beamed. "This is great!" she exclaimed.

Shelly and Adrianna swam over. "I think we found the perfect canvas for our *Starry Night*," Shelly said.

"Follow us!" Adrianna said.

The two girls led everyone to the flat rock Coral had found earlier. Angel scrunched her brow. "But it's too heavy!" she said.

Shelly and Adrianna shook their heads. "It was too heavy for the three of you," Adrianna said, "but like my uncle the mayor likes to say, '*When purrmaids work together, anything is possible!*' With six pairs of paws, we should be strong enough to do anything we want!"

"You're right!" Angel laughed.

The purrmaids arranged their discoveries next to the rock. Coral painted the entire surface blue. "Finally, no rips!" she joked.

Shelly and Umiko glued the shells and sea glass into the shape of Cove Council Hall on one side of the project, while Angel created sea school on the other. Adrianna used the coral pieces to make Tortoiseshell Reef. Cascade used a sharp claw to slice the candy wrapper into a crescent moon. And they all worked together to glue the bottle cap stars onto the blue sky.

As they passed the bottle of snail slime back and forth, Umiko said, "You know, we really didn't mean to cut the line earlier."

Cascade nodded. "We just weren't paying attention."

"And then you guys were so angry," Adrianna said, "that we reacted badly."

Angel felt her face grow hot. "I'm sorry for snapping," she said.

"We are, too," Coral and Shelly echoed.

"We all got off on the wrong paw," Angel said. "I'm glad we started over."

The purrmaids smiled at each other. Then Angel glued the last bottle cap on. "I think we're done!" she purred.

Everyone floated back to take a good look at their project.

"It doesn't look like the Fang Gogh painting," Adrianna said.

"That's because Fang Gogh never saw Kittentail Cove!" Shelly laughed.

"I think this looks paw-some," Coral said.

"Paw-sitively amazing," Umiko added.

"I agree," Cascade said. Then she turned

to Angel. "Thank you for suggesting that we all work together."

"We were actually ready to give up," Adrianna said.

"We couldn't have done this without you," Umiko said. "Or you and you," she added to Coral and Shelly.

Angel grinned. "Well, we couldn't have done it without you, either. But now we really do need each other. Everybody grab an edge. Let's get this thing home!"

The girls lifted the rock. Even with six of them, it was very heavy. "This is harder than I thought it would be," Adrianna panted.

"Don't think about it," Coral answered. "Just lift and swim!"

They carefully passed through the double doors and then down the hallway.

By the time they reached the museum
entryway, they were huffing and puffing.
"Let's take a break," Angel suggested.

She didn't have to tell the other purrmaids twice! They propped the rock against
the wall and sat down on the floor to rest.

"What do you have there?" someone
asked.

Angel turned around. "Mommy!" she cried. She leapt up to hug her mother. "Look at our art project!"

Mayor Rivers and Mrs. Clearwater swam over to look, too. When Mrs. Clearwater saw the creation, her paw went to her heart. "This is incredible, girls!" she said.

"Is this . . . is this *Starry Night*?" Mommy asked.

Angel grinned and said, "I think we would call it *Starry Kittentail Cove*."

"Did you make this out of things from our storeroom?" Mrs. Clearwater asked.

"Yes!" Cascade said. "We found this rock on a shelf and thought it would be perfect as a canvas."

"We used fish oil paint for the background," Umiko said.

"Then Angel had the idea to use things we found in the trash can," Adrianna said. She pointed to the bottle caps and the broken shells and sea glass. "It was a paw-some plan."

"I'm very impressed," Mrs. Clearwater said. "You girls accomplished something that many artists spend their lives trying to do. You saw the beauty in things that get overlooked and found ways to share that beauty with everyone else."

"I'm proud of you," Mommy said, "especially since all *six* of you figured out a way to work together."

The purrmaids beamed. "Now we just have to carry this home," Angel purred.

Mrs. Clearwater blocked their path. "You can't do that," she said, frowning.

"But you said we could use the storeroom stuff for our project!" Angel yelped.

Mrs. Clearwater nodded. "Yes, I did," she said. "And I'm amazed at what you created. But you can't take that out of the museum." She swam to the front entrance. "It's too big to fit through our new door!"

The purrmaids didn't want to believe it. They tried to get the rock through the front door. But no matter how they twisted or turned, their project was too tall and wide.

"I'm so sorry, girls," Mrs. Clearwater purred. "That rock has been in the storage room fur-ever. We did repairs to the museum and replaced the old double doors with this one." She shrugged. "We never thought we'd need to move something that size!"

"What are we going to do about our homework?" Adrianna whined. "Do something, Uncle Ray! You're the *mayor*!"

"I can speak to Ms. Harbor," Mayor Rivers said. "I'll explain what happened. I'm sure she'll understand."

"I'll talk to her, too," Mommy added. "Let's get you girls home, and then I can call her shell phone."

The purrmaids were as quiet as a clam while they swam home. Angel waved goodbye when they dropped off Shelly and Coral but couldn't bring herself to speak.

In the morning, when it was time to get ready for school, Angel was more miserable than usual. She wanted the day to be over before it even started.

"Come on, Angel," Mommy purred. "I told you I talked to Ms. Harbor. She understands what happened."

Angel squeezed her eyes shut and turned her face away. "I still don't want to go to school," she mumbled.

"You *still* have to go," Mommy replied.

Angel, Coral, and Shelly were mostly silent on the swim to sea school. The students in room Eel-Twelve weren't silent, though. Ms. Harbor wasn't in the classroom yet, but everyone else was there. And except for the Catfish Club, everyone else had their art projects.

Some purrmaids had made a sand sculpture of sea school. Another group made a seaweed collage of swimming dolphins.

Baker and Taylor used pages out of an old human book to fold into a collection of shells.

The Catfish Club girls were sitting quietly at their desks. Angel led Shelly and Coral over to them. "Ours was just as good as these," she whispered.

The other girls nodded. "Too bad no one will see it," Umiko mumbled.

"Can I have everyone's attention, please?" Ms. Harbor asked. The purrmaids took their seats. "I know you just got here," she continued, "but we're not staying in class. We have a special appointment this morning!"

"What about our projects?" Baker asked.

"Where are we going?" Taylor asked.

"You'll each get to present your creations," Ms. Harbor said, smiling, "*after* we get back from Kittentail Cove Museum."

Angel's heart sank. That was the last place in the ocean she wanted to go!

When she glanced around, most of the students were smiling. But Shelly, Coral, Adrianna, Umiko, and Cascade all had the same look on their faces—upside-down smiles.

As the class lined up, Angel whispered, "Why do we have to go back to the museum?" Her friends shrugged.

The trip through Kittentail Cove seemed to take forever. Ms. Harbor had to remind Angel to keep up. "I've never seen you swim so slowly!" she said.

Mrs. Clearwater was waiting at the entrance of the museum. "Welcome," she said. "I'm Mrs. Clearwater, the museum director. Ms. Harbor asked me to help with your art lesson today."

"There are so many things you can explore at Kittentail Cove Museum," Ms. Harbor said, "but today we are here to see one thing in particular."

"Follow me," Mrs. Clearwater said. She led the class into the next gallery.

As soon as Angel swam into the room, she froze. "Is that . . . ," she whispered.

Coral and Shelly swam up behind her. Their mouths opened and closed, but nothing came out.

Then the Catfish Club came in. Their eyes grew wide. Adrianna finally broke the silence. "Is that what I think it is?" she asked.

Ms. Harbor and Mrs. Clearwater hovered on either side of a large flat rock. It had been hung in the gallery alongside paintings by Fang Gogh, Picatso, and Furmeer. But the picture on the rock hadn't been created by a famous artist.

"Yesterday, some of your classmates came here to do their homework assignment," Mrs. Clearwater said. "Unfortunately, the project was too big to remove from the museum." She smiled. "But that just means we get to keep this beautiful work by these local Kittentail Cove artists right here on our wall!" She swam over to Angel, Coral, Shelly, and the Catfish Club.

"You guys made this?" Baker asked. "It looks like Kittentail Cove."

"It's fin-tastic!" Taylor added.

"A true masterpiece!" Ms. Harbor declared.

10

"**B**efore you return to sea school," said Mrs. Clearwater, "take a few moments to look through the gallery at the other artwork."

The students happily swam off in all directions, except the six creators of *Starry Kittentail Cove*. They hovered in the same place, staring at their creation.

"I can't believe our work is in a *real* museum," Angel purred.

"That's because it's *real* art." Ms. Harbor laughed. "When Mrs. Shore and Mayor Rivers told me about the size of your problem, I knew there had to be something we could do."

"Then I had the idea to place your work exactly where it belongs!" Mrs. Clearwater said.

"I have a question," Ms. Harbor said. "I'm surprised that the six of you decided to work together. When you left class yesterday, I thought you'd be in two groups of three."

Angel bit her lip. She looked at Coral and Shelly first, and then over at the Catfish Club. No one wanted to be the first to talk, so Angel took a deep breath. "I think I can explain," she began. "Shelly, Coral, and I were planning to work as a group."

"And Umiko, Adrianna, and I were going to work as our own group," Cascade added.

Angel nodded. "We were all here yesterday, and we got a little . . . competitive," she explained.

"Our claws may have come out." Umiko giggled.

"We were working against each other until things got completely out of paw," Angel continued. "But then we realized that what we could make together—"

"Was better than what we could accomplish alone!" Adrianna declared.

Ms. Harbor smiled at them. "You girls learned a great lesson," she said.

"That's because we have a great teacher!" Angel laughed.

"Now, girls, finish admiring your work," Mrs. Clearwater purred. "You have to get back to school soon."

The purrmaids nodded. As soon as the grown-ups were too far away to hear, Angel let out a squeal of delight. "Ms. Harbor loved *Starry Kittentail Cove*!" she exclaimed.

"I was thinking the same thing!" Coral said.

"Me too!" Shelly added.

The Catfish Club girls, though, didn't answer. They were off to the side, whispering to each other. When they finally swam over, they weren't smiling.

"We have to talk to you," Adrianna said.

"We have a bet to settle," Cascade added.

"What?" Angel said, confused. "We worked together!"

"How can there still be a bet?" Shelly asked.

Umiko held up a paw. "We just talked about it, and we think there's a pretty clear winner here."

"Angel, you're the reason we even have a project to show today," Adrianna said.

"Your idea was the best," Umiko added, "so you win."

"The three of you didn't need to let us work with you," Cascade said. "You could have created *Starry Kittentail Cove* without our help."

Angel shook her head, but Adrianna stopped her. "Cascade is right," she said.

"I'm right a lot." Cascade giggled.

"We want you guys to have these," Umiko explained.

Each girl took a pearl off her necklace and held it out.

"There's one for each of you," Cascade said. "We thought maybe you could wear them on your bracelets."

Angel looked from Coral to Shelly. She was so surprised! "I don't know what to say," she mumbled.

Adrianna giggled. "As my uncle the mayor would say, *'Just say, Thank you.'*"

Angel, Coral, and Shelly each clipped the lavender pearls to their bracelets. "Thank you," Shelly purred. Coral and Angel nodded.

"You guys were the best this time," Umiko admitted.

"We'll see what happens next time," Cascade added.

"Yes, we will!" Angel laughed. She knew there would be a next time with the Catfish Club—and she was looking forward to it!